W9-CIB-419

World of Reading

LEVEL 1

MARVEL

THESE ARE THE MARVEL SUPER HEROES

Copyright © 2022 MARVEL

This Is Black Widow adapted by Elana Cohen. Illustrated by Michela Frare. Painted by Angela Capolugo.
Based on the Marvel comic book character Black Widow. Copyright © 2020 MARVEL.

This Is Captain Marvel adapted by Kelsey Sullivan. Illustrated by Cucca Vincenzo and
Salvatore Di Marco. Painted by Stefani Rennee, Anna Beliashova, and Vita Efremova.
Based on the Marvel comic book character Captain Marvel. Copyright © 2019 MARVEL.

This Is Miles Morales adapted by Alexandra West. Illustrated by Aurelio Mazzara and Gaetano Petrigno. Painted
by Jay David Ramos. Based on the Marvel comic book character Miles Morales. Copyright © 2018 MARVEL.

This Is Black Panther adapted by Alexandra West. Illustrated by Simone Boufantino, Davide Mastrolondardo,
and Fabio Paciulli. Based on the Marvel comic book character Black Panther. Copyright © 2018 MARVEL.

This Is Thor adapted by Alexandra West. Illustrated by Roberto Di Salvo, Simone Boufantino, and
Tomasso Moscardini. Based on the Marvel comic book character Thor. Copyright © 2017 MARVEL.

This Is Doctor Strange adapted by Alexandra West. Illustrated by Simone Di Meo, Mario Del Pennino, and
Tommaso Moscardini. Based on the Marvel comic book character Doctor Strange. Copyright © 2016 MARVEL.

All rights reserved. Published by Marvel Press, an imprint of Buena Vista Books, Inc.
No part of this book may be reproduced or transmitted in any form or by any means, electronic or
mechanical, including photocopying, recording, or by any information storage and retrieval system,
without written permission from the publisher. For information address Marvel Press,
77 West 66th Street, New York, New York 10023.

ISBN 978-1-368-06199-5
FAC-025393-22045

Printed in Guangdong, China
First Hardcover Edition, February 2022
1 3 5 7 9 10 8 6 4 2

MARVEL

BLACK WIDOW

THIS IS BLACK WIDOW

Adapted by **Elana Cohen**

Illustrated by **Michela Frare**

Painted by **Angela Capolugo**

Based on the Marvel comic book character **Black Widow**

MARVEL

Los Angeles
New York

This is Natasha Romanoff.
She is Black Widow.

Black Widow is very strong.
She is fast.
She is smart.

Natasha grows up in Russia.
She is trained as a secret agent
in the Red Room.

Natasha is special.
She is the best of all the girls.

Natasha gets older.
She becomes a secret agent.

She becomes Black Widow.

But Black Widow does not always want to fight.

One day on a mission,
Black Widow must battle a
Super Hero named Hawkeye.

Hawkeye and Black Widow become friends.
Hawkeye convinces Black Widow to lead a better life.

Black Widow and Hawkeye
begin to work for Nick Fury
and S.H.I.E.L.D.

Now Black Widow is an Avenger!

As an Avenger, Black Widow fights many Super Villains alongside her team.

The team lives in Avengers Tower.

Nick Fury tells Black Widow about a new threat. There is a threat in Russia. The threat is an impostor Black Widow.

Black Widow travels with Fury
to investigate the impostor.

The impostor knows that Black Widow and Fury are coming.

The impostor Black Widow plans to tell them to leave her alone. She has work to do.

Natasha wants to keep people safe. But the impostor Black Widow escapes.

Who is she?

The two Black Widows meet again.
Natasha discovers the truth.
The other impostor is Yelena Belova.

Yelena grew up with Natasha in the Red Room.
Natasha and Yelena were friends.

Natasha wants Yelena to
stop doing bad things.

She wants them to be
friends again.

Yelena has a mission she needs
to complete.
She does not want to stop.
She fights Natasha and
escapes again.

Black Widow wants to
search for Yelena.
But the team needs her to
return home.

Black Widow and Nick Fury
board the plane.
There are other villains to fight.

Black Widow will not forget Yelena. Maybe one day, she will find Yelena again.

Black Widow is a Super Hero!

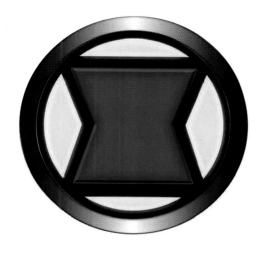

THIS IS CAPTAIN MARVEL

Adapted by **Kelsey Sullivan**

Illustrated by **Cucca Vincenzo** *and* **Salvatore Di Marco**

Painted by **Stefani Rennee, Anna Beliashova,** *and* **Vita Efremova**

Based on the Marvel comic book character **Captain Marvel**

Los Angeles
New York

This is Carol Danvers.
She is Captain Marvel.

Carol Danvers
is a pilot.

She is a part of
the US Air Force.

For the safety of the planet,
Carol must meet with
the Kree alien race.

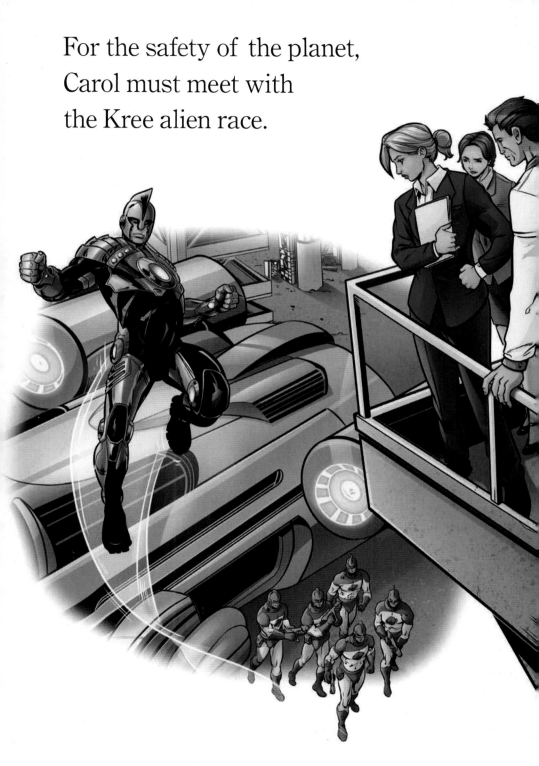

During the meeting,
a Kree device explodes.

Carol is caught
in the blast.

The explosion gives Carol super-powers. She can float!

She can fly through the air
by just thinking about it.

She can shoot
energy from her hands
by tightening her fists.

She is strong.
She is fast.
She is Captain Marvel.

She uses her
powers for good.

Captain Marvel
explores space.

Captain Marvel saves
the world.

Captain Marvel always
protects her home, the Earth.

Captain Marvel joins the
Alpha Flight Space Program.

Alpha Flight gets attacked by alien robots.

The robots attack
the computers.

Captain Marvel
blasts them with energy.

Captain Marvel protects Earth against an alien invasion.

Captain Marvel teams up
with the Avengers.

The missions take her all over the world and through the cosmos.

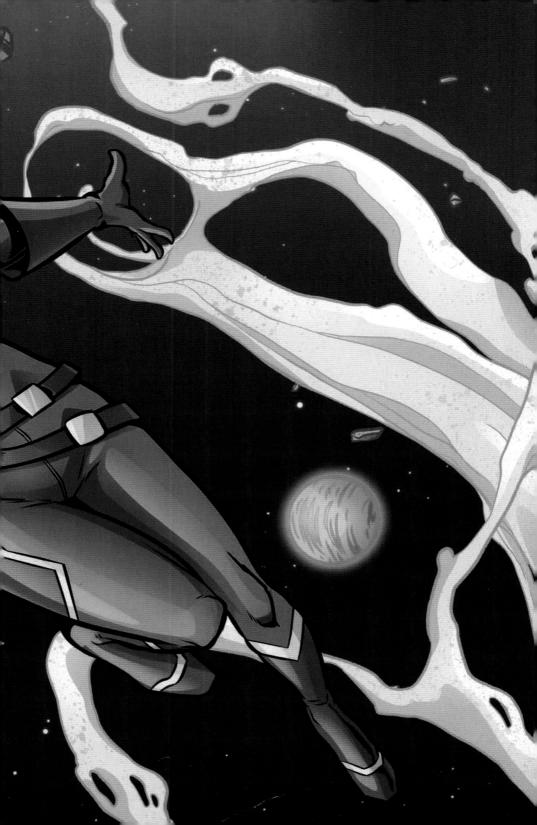

Captain Marvel
is a Super Hero!

MARVEL

SPIDER-MAN

THIS IS MILES MORALES

Adapted by Alexandra West

Illustrated by Aurelio Mazzara *and* Gaetano Petrigno

Painted by Jay David Ramos

Based on the Marvel comic book character Miles Morales

MARVEL

Los Angeles
New York

This is Miles Morales.

Miles Morales
lives in New York.

He is a
normal kid.

Miles Morales goes to school.

He is very smart.

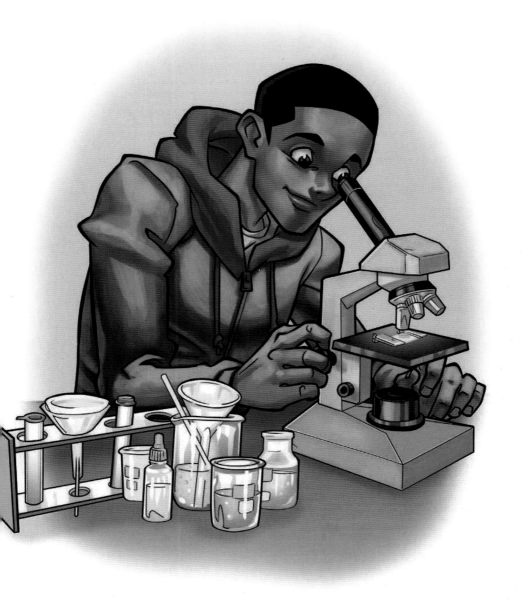

Miles has many friends.

He is friends
with Peter Parker.

Miles does not know that
Peter Parker is Spider-Man!

One day, Miles follows
Peter Parker.

He does not
notice the spider!

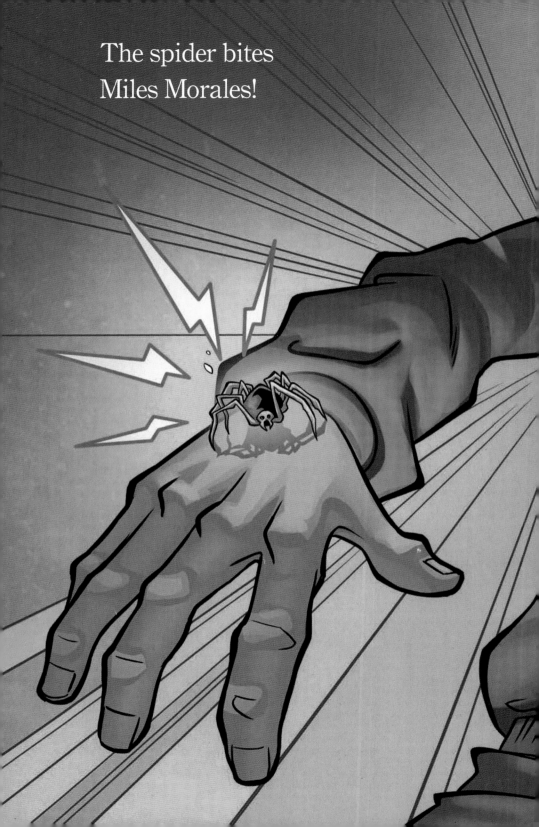

Miles gets super powers.

Miles gets spider powers!

Miles can do
everything Peter can do.

He is strong.

Miles can climb.

Miles can shoot webs.

Miles can swing
through the city.

Miles has spidey senses.

Miles can also do
things Peter cannot.

He has a venom strike.

He can blend in.

Miles uses his
powers for good.

Miles and Peter
work together.

They fight villains!

Miles and Peter defeat
villains!

Miles Morales is
a Super Hero!

He helps Peter Parker protect the city.

Miles Morales
is Spider-Man!

© 2022 MARVEL

MARVEL

BLACK PANTHER

THIS IS BLACK PANTHER

Adapted by Alexandra West

Illustrated by Simone Boufantino, David Mastrolondardo, *and* Fabio Paciulli

Based on the Marvel comic book character Black Panther

Los Angeles
New York

This is Black Panther.

Long ago, Bashenga was
the first Black Panther.

Black Panther is a
very important role.

Black Panther wears a suit.
He has super abilities.
He protects Wakanda.

Wakanda is a country.
It is in Africa.
It has many resources.

T'Chaka is the Black Panther.
He has a family.
Ramonda is his wife.
T'Challa is his son.

T'Challa grows up.
He works hard.
T'Challa wants to be
just like his father.

One day, a villain
steals from Wakanda.
His name is Klaw.

Klaw gets away.

Black Panther tracks Klaw.
He catches the villain.
T'Challa follows.

Klaw attacks Black Panther.
T'Challa shields himself.
But Black Panther is hurt!

T'Challa tries
to fight Klaw.

Klaw escapes.
T'Challa holds his father.
T'Challa is very sad.

T'Challa will avenge his father.
He will become Black Panther.

T'Challa puts on his father's suit.
He needs to find Klaw.

T'Challa finds Klaw.
They are both ready to fight!

Klaw is strong.
He knocks T'Challa
to the ground.

T'Challa is stronger.
He kicks Klaw.
Klaw flies through the air.

T'Challa jumps.
T'Challa lands.
T'Challa defeats Klaw!

T'Challa returns to Wakanda.
He kneels before his mother.
She crowns him.

T'Challa is crowned
the new Black Panther.
Everyone cheers!

Like his father, Black Panther
will protect Wakanda.
But he must also protect the world.

Black Panther becomes a Super Hero.

T'Challa is Black Panther!

World of Reading

MARVEL
THE MIGHTY THOR

THIS IS THOR

Adapted by **Alexandra West**

Illustrated by **Roberto Di Salvo, Simone Boufantino,**
and **Tomasso Moscardini**

Based on the Marvel comic book character **Thor**

Los Angeles
New York

This is Thor.

Thor lives on Asgard.
It is a planet in space.

Thor and Loki are
the sons of King Odin.
They grow up together.

King Odin makes a
magic hammer.
The hammer is for Thor.

Thor is the favorite son.
Loki is jealous of Thor.

The hammer is heavy.
Thor cannot lift the hammer.
Only a person who is
worthy can lift it.

Thor works hard
to be worthy.

Thor fights great beasts.
He shows he can be brave.

Thor fights big monsters.
He shows he can be strong.

Thor tries again.
He lifts the hammer.
Thor is finally worthy!

Thor throws his hammer.
It flies back to him.

Thor stamps his hammer
on the ground.

Thor twirls his hammer
to fly through the sky.

Thor shows off his power.
He is very selfish.

King Odin sees Thor.
He is very angry.

King Odin curses
Thor to live on Earth.

Thor must be a human.
His name is Don Blake.
He is a doctor.

Don Blake helps people.
He finds his hammer.
Don Blake becomes Thor!
The curse is broken.

Thor has his powers back.
He is the Mighty Thor.

Loki learns dark magic.
He is evil.
He sees Thor on Earth.
Loki has an idea.

Loki makes Hulk angry.
Hulk attacks Thor.

Thor fights back!
He realizes Loki
tricked Hulk.

Thor decides to be
a force for good.
He will defeat evil.

Thor has an idea.
He flies away.

Thor cannot defeat
evil alone.
He joins a team.
He joins the Avengers!

Thor is the Mighty Avenger.

MARVEL

DOCTOR STRANGE

THIS IS DOCTOR STRANGE

Adapted by **Alexandra West**

Illustrated by **Simone Di Meo, Mario Del Pennino,**
and **Tomasso Moscardini**

Based on the Marvel comic book character **Doctor Strange**

MARVEL

Los Angeles
New York

This is Stephen Strange.

Stephen is also Doctor Strange.
Doctor Strange is a Super Hero!

Stephen was not always
Doctor Strange.
He was once a surgeon.

Surgeons use their hands to help people.
Stephen's hands were strong and steady.

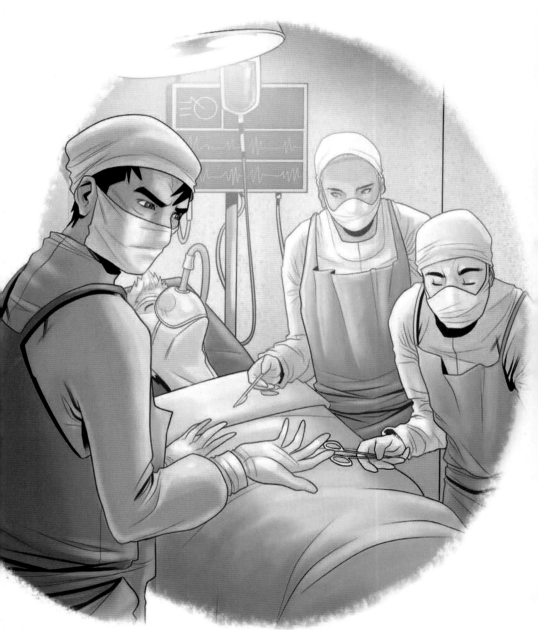

Stephen liked what he did.
He made people feel better.

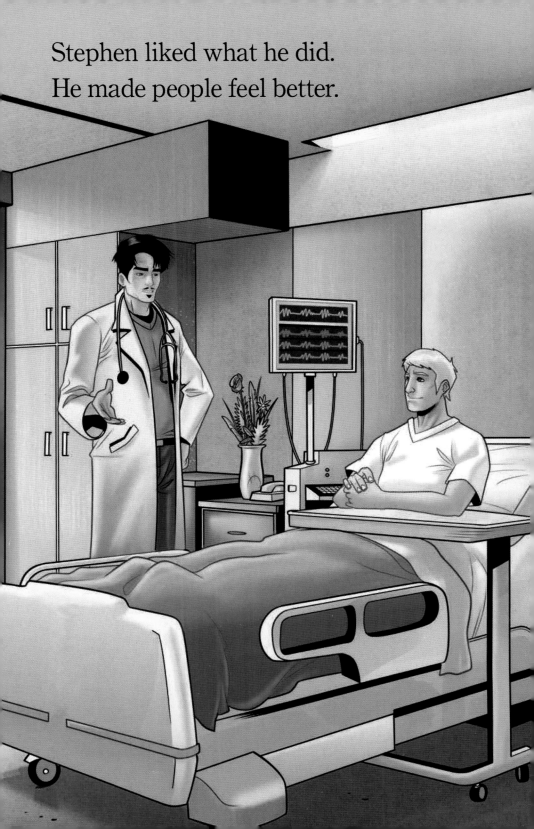

One day, Stephen was in an accident.
His hands were hurt.
Stephen was told his hands would
never get better.
That made Stephen sad.

Stephen needed to fix his hands.
He went away for help.
He went to another country.

A man told Stephen about magic.
Magic would fix his hands.
He would find magic in Tibet.

Stephen arrived in Tibet. Stephen saw someone being attacked.

Stephen had to protect
the man.

Stephen scared away the
thugs. Stephen saved the man.

The man Stephen helped was called the Ancient One. The Ancient One was thankful. He decided to help Stephen.

Stephen started his training in magic.
Stephen worked hard.
He felt the magic healing his hands.

Stephen became very good at magic!
Stephen became Doctor Strange!

Doctor Strange lives in New York City.

Doctor Strange is a
master of the mystic arts.

Doctor Strange is always busy.
People near and far ask for his help.

They know Doctor Strange
will save them.

Doctor Strange can float.

Doctor Strange has many magical tools.
His tools help him fight the bad guys!

Doctor Strange
uses spell books.
He uses a book
of good spells.

Doctor Strange casts spells.
Doctor Strange saves people
from danger.

Doctor Strange has a magical charm.
The charm has many powers.

It can help Doctor Strange see through illusions.

Doctor Strange has a best friend.
His name is Wong.

Wong teaches Doctor
Strange how to fight.

Doctor Strange fights Super Villains.
He protects the planet from evil!

Doctor Strange has lots
of powerful friends.

Together they fight bad guys. They make a great team.

Doctor Strange
helps save the day!

Doctor Strange
is a hero!